THE CURSE OF THE SCAREWOLF

FOR BELLA CORNICHOUNE AND COCO VAN DUSEN

Scholastic Canada Ltd.
604 King Street West, Toronto, Ontario M5V 1E1, Canada

Scholastic Inc.
557 Broadway, New York, NY 10012, USA

Scholastic Australia Pty Limited
PO Box 579, Gosford, NSW 2250, Australia

Scholastic New Zealand Limited
Private Bag 94407, Botany, Manukau 2163, New Zealand

Scholastic Children's Books
Euston House, 24 Eversholt Street, London NW1 1DB, UK

www.scholastic.ca

Library and Archives Canada Cataloguing in Publication

Title: The curse of the scarewolf / Dom Pelletier;
English text by Dina Ginzburg
Other titles: Rodri-Garou. English
Names: Pelletier, Dominique, author, artist. | Ginzburg, Dina, translator.
Description: Series statement: The lunch club | Translation of: Le Rodri-Garou.
Identifiers: Canadiana 20210098805 | ISBN 9781443182720 (softcover)
Subjects: LCGFT: Graphic novels.
Classification: LCC PN6733.P45 R6313 2021 | DDC j741.5/971—dc23

6 5 4 3 2 1 Printed in China 62 21 22 23 24 25

DOM PELLETIER

THE CURSE OF THE SCAREWOLF

ENGLISH TEXT BY DINA GINZBURG

Scholastic Canada Ltd.

Toronto New York London Auckland Sydney
Mexico City New Delhi Hong Kong Buenos Aires

PLEASANT VALLEY ELEMENTARY

PLEASANT VALLEY ELEMENTARY

SCHOOL MAP

HEH
HEH
HEH!

SCIENCE FAIR
HALLOWEEN
PARTY

A FEW HOURS LATER...
SCHOOL BUS

MORNING!
HEY...

SO, DO YOU THINK EVERYTHING IS READY?
YEAH.
YEAH.

BUT I STILL THINK IT'S A BAD IDEA...

NO WAY, IT'LL BE GREAT! YOU'LL SEE. WHO DOESN'T LOVE STAMPS?
HALLOWEEN
PARTY
IF YOU SAY SO.

HEY THERE, LUNCH CLUBBERS! IT'S THE BIG DAY.
HI, MR. PEABODY!
GRUMBLE
GUESS WHAT I BROUGHT?
ALWAYS WITH THE STAMPS...

LET'S GO, SLOWPOKES! WE'RE GOING TO BE LATE!

STAMPS
SC
RECYCLING
MOON ROCKS
FLU

ENCE FAIR
STAMPS
GRRR!
VOLCANOES
RO

JUST LIKE I THOUGHT. THIS IS SO UNCOOL! WE'RE SHOWING OFF DUSTY, BORING OLD STAMPS.

ARE THEY EVEN SCIENCE? THERE'S SO MUCH AMAZING STUFF IN THE LUNCH CLUB'S HIDEOUT. IMAGINE WHAT WE COULD HAVE SHOWN!
HEY THERE!
STAMPS
LEO'S SO COOL!
BUT NOOO, WE HAVE TO KEEP IT UNDER THE RADAR.

NOBODY'S GOING TO CHECK OUT OUR BOOTH.
Z
Z
Z
Z
Z

DON'T TOUCH THAT! YOU'LL WRECK IT!

STA
IN FACT, DON'T EVEN LOOK AT THEM!
WEIRDO.

I THINK I FIGURED OUT WHY WE'RE NOT POPULAR.

THIS IS SO BORING! I'M GOING TO CHECK OUT THE OTHER BOOTHS.

EVEN THESE DUSTY OLD ROCKS ARE MORE EXCITING THAN STAMPS.

POTATO CLOCK
MY SPUD!
MMM... NOT BAD.

VOLCANOES

STAMPS
LET'S GO, "MR. SCIENCE." YOU KNOW WHERE.
PRINCIPAL
SEE YOU GUYS BACK AT THE CLUB. IT'S DETENTION TIME.
CALL MY LAWYER!
A LITTLE LATER THAT DAY...
THAT WAS THE BEST SCIENCE FAIR EVER!
MY PRECIOUS STAMPS.
HELLO, MR. BOB!
HELLO, TIA! I SEE YOU'RE HEADING BACK TO LOCK UP THOSE STAMPS. BETTER KEEP THEM SAFE!

NO PROBLEM. THERE ARE PLENTY OF DISGUISES IN OUR SECRET HIDEOUT!

SWISH
CLICK

SECRET HIDEOUT

THERE REALLY IS EVERYTHING HERE!
WE EVEN HAVE A REAL SUIT OF MEDIEVAL ARMOUR!
AUTHENTIC PLASTIC!

THIS LOOKS LIKE THE EVIL ALIEN ZARALGAX'S CAPE!
IT SURE DOES. WHAT AN ADVENTURE THAT WAS!
I REMEMBER IT LIKE IT WAS YESTERDAY...
I WAS SO YOUNG.
IT WAS LITERALLY ONE MONTH AGO.*
*SEE BOOK 1

ROBIN HOOD! THIS ONE IS PERFECT!
THE TIGHTS ARE COMFY AND GENTEEL.*
THESE ARE AWESOME, BUT I'M GOING TO STICK WITH MY FIRST CHOICE... THE COSTUME I BROUGHT FROM HOME!
IT'S KNIT FROM REAL UNICORN HAIR!

WHAT ABOUT YOU, MR. PEABODY?
WHAT'S YOUR COSTUME?
ME? WAIT FOR IT...I'M DRESSING UP AS...AS...
*LOOK IT UP. I'M NOT GOING TO EXPLAIN **EVERYTHING.**

AGAIN?
Z Z Z Z Z Z
PIC PIC

WHY DOES HE KEEP FALLING ASLEEP?
WHATEVER. WE NEED TO GET GOING.

I NEVER SLEEP!
?
? ?

WHY DO YOU TAKE SO MANY NAPS?
PSST... IT'S BECAUSE HE'S OLD. HE'S AT LEAST FORTY.

WHY DO I SOMETIMES TAKE LITTLE BREAKS? BUT...BUT THE ANSWER'S IN *THE JOY OF STAMPS*!
?
YOU'VE READ IT, RIGHT? RIGHT?!
THE JOY OF STAMPS

UH...
SORRY, BUT...UM...AH...OH! MY INTERNATIONAL MODELLING CAREER DOESN'T LEAVE ME WITH A LOT OF TIME RIGHT NOW.
KIDS THESE DAYS...

WHY, THIS BOOK IS A MUST-READ! PART ONE IS BURSTING WITH INFORMATION ABOUT STAMPS, PLUS ADVICE FOR FIGHTING THE EVILEST OF ADVERSARIES, FROM ANCHOVIES TO ZOMBIES...
ALL IN PERFECT ALPHABETICAL ORDER, COMPLETE WITH LOVELY ILLUSTRATIONS.

ACTUALLY, THAT SOUNDS PRETTY COOL.
AND IT GETS EVEN BETTER IN PART TWO, AN EPIC TELLING OF OUR CLUB'S HISTORY, FROM ITS ORIGINS ALL THE WAY TO MODERN TIMES.
WAIT, THERE'S PICTURES?

LET'S SEE HERE...LAGOON CREATURES... THE ONE-CENT MAGENTA...VAMPIRES...AH! PART TWO, CHAPTER ONE: THE FOUNDING OF OUR BELOVED CLUB...
SINCE WHEN DO WE HAVE A FIREPLACE?

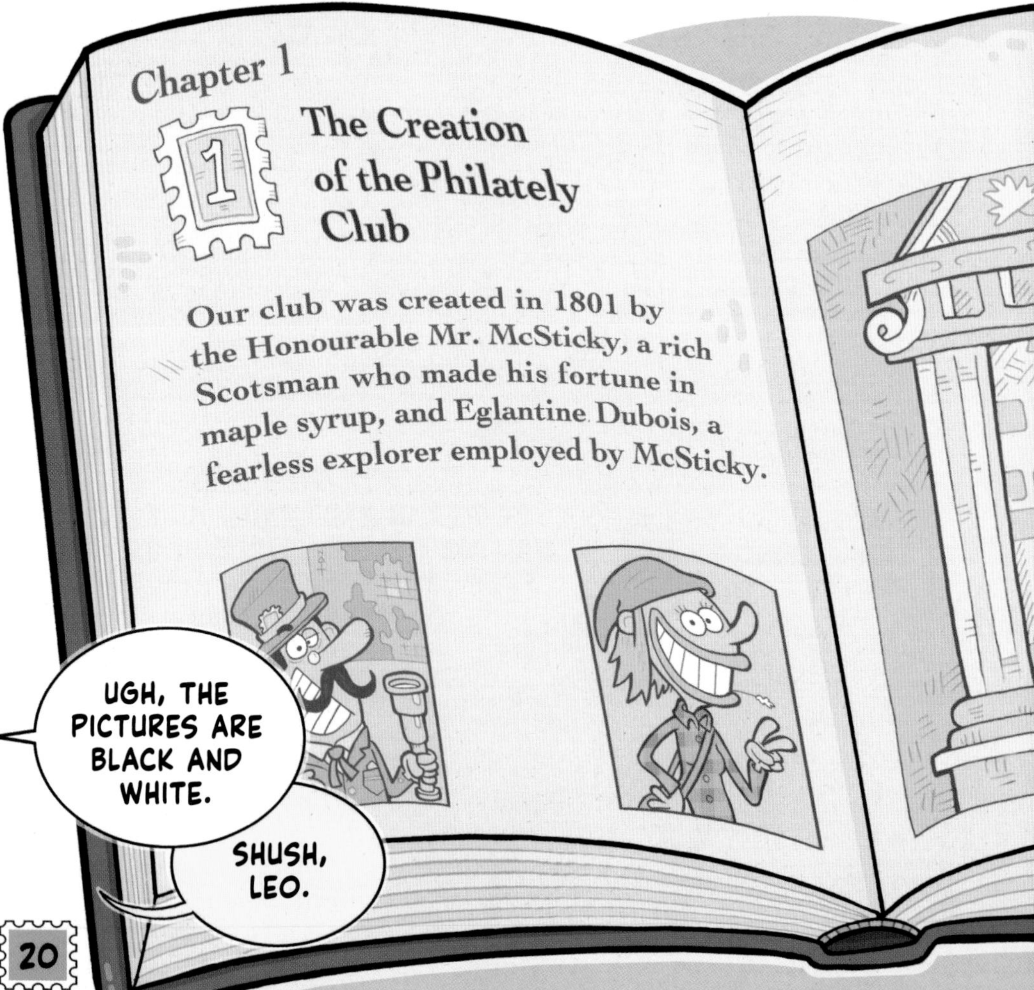
Chapter 1
1
The Creation of the Philately Club
Our club was created in 1801 by the Honourable Mr. McSticky, a rich Scotsman who made his fortune in maple syrup, and Eglantine Dubois, a fearless explorer employed by McSticky.
UGH, THE PICTURES ARE BLACK AND WHITE.
SHUSH, LEO.

After an arduous, sandwichless journey braving the elements Ms. Dubois had discovered...

...A NEW ROUTE FOR EXPORTING MAPLE SYRUP TO THE SOUTH!
$

CONGRATULATIONS, MS. DUBOIS! THANKS TO YOU, THE EXPORTATION OF MAPLE SYRUP WILL BE REVOLUTIONIZED!

THIS IS A **MOMENTOUS** OCCASION. LET US CELEBRATE!
A DROP OF SYRUP?

I ENVY YOU, DEAR EGLANTINE! IT WILL BE A NEW ADVENTURE EVERY DAY.
COLD! DANGER! BLACKFLIES! IT'S ALL SO VERY **EXCITING!**

YOU KNOW, YOU CAN ALWAYS COME WITH ME.
WHAT A GRAND IDEA!
WITH MY MONEY AND YOUR TALENT, WE WILL HAVE **IMMENSE** AMOUNTS OF FUN...
AND SO BEGINS THE ADVENTURES OF EGLANTINE AND McSTICKY!

AH, BERTRAND, MY GOOD AND FAITHFUL SERVANT. I AM GOING ON AN ADVENTURE! YOU WILL TAKE CARE OF THE DETAILS FOR ME.
VERY GOOD, SIR.
WOULD SIR LIKE ME TO PREPARE SIR A SANDWICH FOR THE ROAD?

HA HA! MY INNOCENT AND NAIVE BERTRAND, DANGER WILL BE MY ONLY SUSTENANCE.
PREPARE INSTEAD A SUITCASE FULL OF CASH!
PAT PAT

McS
EXPORTS
AH, ADVENTURE... IT'S **ENTHRALLING!** WHAT DO WE DO FIRST?
SHOULD WE GRAB A BITE? I'M FEELING A BIT PECKISH.

DESPITE RATHER ROUGH BEGINNINGS...
SO THIS IS NATURE.
HUH. IT'S GREENER THAN I HAD IMAGINED.

DEARY ME. WE'LL NEED TO GO BACK. I FORGOT TO BRING MY SPARE MONOCLE.

...EGLANTINE AND MCSTICKY MADE QUITE THE TEAM...

...AND WHILE THEIR ADVENTURES WERE AT FIRST MODEST IN NATURE...

...OUR INTREPID ADVENTURERS SOON BECAME KNOWN FOR THEIR DERRING-DO.

$
YOU CAPTURED MARKY MALICIOUS? WELL DONE! HE'S BEEN ON THE RUN FOR MONTHS!
GRR
PRISON
WANTED
$50

YOU SAVED OUR VILLAGE FROM THE BEAVER INVASION!
WE'RE POSITIVELY POPULAR.
I'VE GOT A **CRACKING** IDEA!

GRAND OPENiNG
THE McSTICKY & DUBOIS AGENCY
SOLUTIONS FOR ANY OCCASION
WHAT A COLOSSAL CROWD!
SO MANY POTENTIAL CUSTOMERS!
BRAVO
HURRAH!

BUT WHAT HAD SEEMED LIKE A GOOD IDEA...
YOU SAY THERE'S GHOSTS IN THE GRAVEYARD?
NO TROUBLE AT ALL!

A GIANT CROCODILE IN YOUR TOILET?
WE'LL CRACK THE CASE!
OUCHIE...

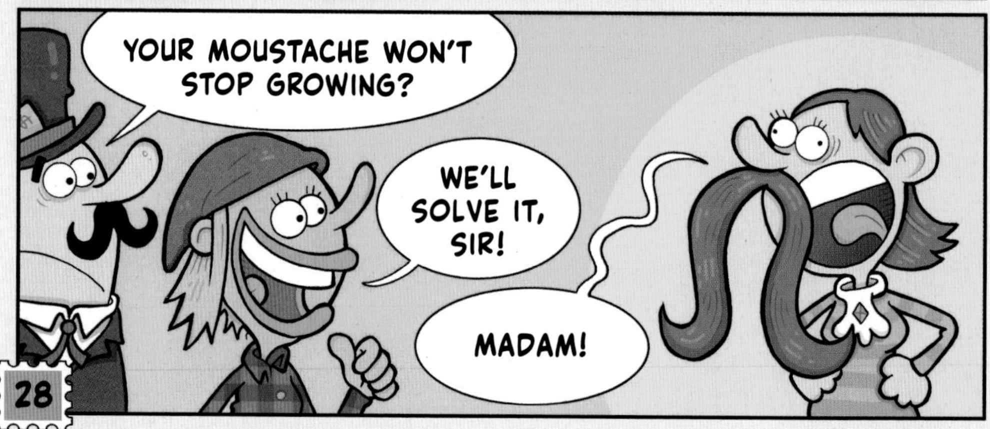
YOUR MOUSTACHE WON'T STOP GROWING?
WE'LL SOLVE IT, SIR!
MADAM!

...PRETTY QUICKLY...
LOST OBJECTS
FAKE MONSTERS
HUFFY HENS
BALDNESS
COLD SOUP
OH DEAR. OUR LIST OF "PROBLEMS" TO SOLVE IS BECOMING LONGER AND LONGER. AND SMALLER AND SMALLER IN THE ACTUAL DERRING-DO DEPARTMENT.

...BECAME AN IDEA WITH UNFORESEEN AND TERRIBLE CONSEQUENCES.
THE McSTICKY & DUBOIS AGENCY
SOLUTIONS FOR ANY OCCASION
FOR THE TENTH TIME, YOUR CHICKEN IS NOT POSSESSED.
YOU'VE BEEN HERE EVERY DAY THIS WEEK.
SO MANY PEOPLE!
TOO MANY PEOPLE.
THEY REFUSED TO HELP ME!
CLUCK CLUCK
SHAME ON THEM!
IT'S A SCANDAL, I SAY!
WE DEMAND A REFUND!
CLUCK CLUCK
COME OUT!
BOO!
GRRR!

THESE PEOPLE ARE OUT OF CONTROL.
I'D RATHER FACE A HERD OF RABID RABBITS!
I SIMPLY WANTED TO MAKE A BIT OF MONEY... UH...I MEAN, DO SOME GOOD!
KNOCK
KNOCK
KNOCK
DO YOU HAVE A VALID PERMIT?
I'LL SEE YOU IN COURT.
THIS IS A JOB FOR THE POLICE.
THEY'RE AGENTS OF EVIL!
FOR THE RECORD, ARE YOU ALIENS?
CLUCK CLUCK

THE SITUATION BECOMING UNBEARABLE, EGLANTINE AND McSTICKY CLOSED THEIR DOORS...

GOODBYE
(FOREVER!)

GOOD RIDDANCE!
GOODBYE
(FOREVER!)

SUCH A SHAME. WE ONLY WANTED TO SAVE THE WORLD! AND MAKE MONEY.
BUT MAYBE WE STILL CAN.

WE CAN STILL SAVE THE WORLD--IN SECRET, SO NOBODY WILL BOTHER US!
AND WE CAN STILL MAKE MONEY!

BUT HOW WILL WE KEEP IT ON THE DOWN-LOW?
WE CAN HARDLY HIDE OUT IN THE WOODS!
I HAVE AN IDEA!

WE'LL CREATE A CLUB SO UNCOOL NOBODY WILL WANT TO JOIN!
EXCELLENT!

BUT WHAT KIND OF CLUB IS SO BORING THAT EVERYONE WOULD IGNORE IT?
A BROCCOLI LOVERS' CLUB?
MINERALOGY?
COLLECTORS OF MACARONI NECKLACES?
OF BELLY-BUTTON FLUFF?

I'VE GOT IT! A PHILATELY CLUB! YOU KNOW, STAMP COLLECTING.
NOBODY WOULD WANT TO JOIN A STAMP COLLECTING CLUB.

BUT I ACTUALLY LIKE STAMPS!
PERFECT! IT'S ALL SETTLED THEN.

AND THAT, DEAR READER, IS HOW THE PHILATELY CLUB CAME TO BE.
PHILATELY CLUB
SPLENDID! WE CAN HAVE THE STAMPS ALL TO OURSELVES.
DECENT DIGS!
THERE'S NO ONE HERE TO BOTHER US!
STAMPS? WEIRDOS!
HEE HEE!

AND THERE YOU HAVE IT. WHY WE MEET AT LUNCH IS, OF COURSE, ANOTHER STORY.
BUT I WANT TO FIND OUT NOW.
I CAN'T BELIEVE I JUST SAID THAT.
Philately

ANOTHER TIME. YOU NEED TO GET GOING TO THE HALLOWEEN PARTY!
I'LL GET READY AND MEET YOU THERE.

I CAN'T WAIT TO SEE MR. PEABODY'S COSTUME.
MY FAMILY'S COMING DRESSED UP TOO. YOU'LL GET TO MEET THEM!
Philately Club

HEE HEE!
I CAN'T WAIT TO SEE THEIR FACES WHEN THEY SEE ME...

...ALL DRESSED UP IN MY BEST...

...GORILLA SUIT!
PEOPLE LOVE GORILLAS!

WAIT A MINUTE.
HMM. AM I TOO OLD TO DRESS UP FOR HALLOWEEN?

MMM...CANDY...
NO! YOU'RE NEVER TOO OLD FOR CANDY!

POKE!

OUCH!

UGH. I DON'T FEEL VERY...
GOOD.
BANG!

RATZRULE TO TURNIPYUK: ALL GOOD! THE PLAN IS A GO!

ARGHLB

CRACK!

GRRRR

ROARRRRRRR
YES! IT'S WORKING!
HEH
HEH
HEH

THIS TRANSFORMATION IS BROUGHT TO YOU BY:
INSTAFAST SCAREWOLF SERUM*
*AVAILABLE NOWHERE!
RATZRULE TO TURNIPYUK, COME IN. PHASE ONE COMPLETE.
INITIATING PHASE TWO. TURNIPYUK, CONFIRM.
OK!
HEY, YOU! SCAREWOLF. YES, YOU.

CAN YOU HEAR ME? DO YOU UNDERSTAND?
AWOOOO!
RIGHT. I'LL TAKE THAT AS A YES...

PAY ATTENTION! FIRST, YOU WILL BITE TIA AND LEO...
...THEN, YOU CAN DO WHATEVER YOU WANT.

BUT DON'T FORGET TIA AND LEO!

YIKES!

GRRR

GRRR
GNAP!
GRRRR
GRRRRRBL!

Philately
Club

?
?

?

BAAAAA!

BIG HALLOWEEN BASH

COSTUME CONTEST

HEY, WONDER MOM!

TIA, THESE ARE MY PARENTS AND MY BROTHER, GUS.
LOVELY TO MEET YOU.

HELLO, TIA. LEO HAS TOLD US SO MUCH ABOUT YOU!
GA!

I'M NEW THIS YEAR. HE'S PRETTY MUCH MY BEST FRIEND.

YOU KNOW, WE FIRST MET BACK WHEN WE WERE IN SCHOOL.
IT WAS LOVE AT FIRST SIGHT!
GUV!
?
GOOD EVENING, GHOSTS, GHOULS AND GOBLINS!
NOT A CHANCE!
NOT AT ALL!

WELCOME TO PLEASANT VALLEY ELEMENTARY'S BIG HALLOWEEN BASH!

AS PRINCIPAL OF PLEASANT VALLEY ELEMENTARY, IT GIVES ME GREAT PLEASURE TO--
GRBL!
...UH, TO...
GRRRRRR

AWOOOOOO!

AHHHHHHHHH!

HA HA HA!
HA!
BRAVO!
COOL SPECIAL EFFECTS!
HA!
I WAS ALMOST SCARED!
LET'S DANCE!
HA!
TOTALLY REALISTIC!

BIG HALLOWEEN
AHHHHHHHH!

DID THAT WEREWOLF LOOK SORT OF FAMILIAR?
YEAH. THAT BOW TIE REMINDED ME OF...

MR. PEABODY?
RIGHT?! BUT HOW? WHY? WHEN? WHERE?

HE TOOK OFF TOWARDS THE WOODS...
QUICK! LET'S FOLLOW HIM!
HEY--WE'RE GONNA GO FOR A WALK...
AWWW! AREN'T THEY CUTE?
LOOK, A DANCING PUMPKIN!

WHOSE GREAT IDEA WAS IT TO PUT A SUPER-CREEPY FOREST RIGHT BEHIND OUR SCHOOL?

YOU ARE THE WORST WEREWOLF IN THE WORLD!
SHH...

THE PLAN WAS SIMPLE. NO ONE WOULD HAVE NOTICED A WEREWOLF ON HALLOWEEN. ALL YOU HAD TO DO WAS BITE THOSE KIDS...
...NOT THE PRINCIPAL!
HMMM. MAYBE THE INSTAFAST SCAREWOLF SERUM WORKED A LITTLE TOO WELL. THAT SHEEP COSTUME WAS PRETTY CONVINCING.
FINE! YES, YOU CAN BITE HER, BUT DO IT QUIETLY. CAN'T YOU SEE I'M TRYING TO SET UP MY HOLOPHONE?

BEEP!
BOOP!
AH! IT'S WORKING.

HELLO, PIZZA ROYALE. WHAT IS YOUR ORDER?

OHH! I'D LIKE A PIZZA WITH TRIPLE CHEESE!

UH...I MEAN...SORRY, WRONG NUMBER.
CLICK

STUPID PHONE, COME ON! HOW DO I GET THE PICTURE?
BZZZOT

NICE TO SEE YOU, ZARALGAX. I'M IN THE WOODS WITH MR. PEABODY. ERR, I MEAN THE SCAREWOLF.
DUH! I CAN SEE THAT.
? ?? ??
I'M RIGHT ABOVE YOU, IN THE SPACE TURNIP!

THEN WHY NOT COME DOWN AND HELP?
I ALREADY TOLD YOU, MOUSE!
I'M A RAT!

IT'S THOSE MEDDLING KIDS, TIA AND LEO. THEY KNOW ABOUT MY ALLERGY. I'M JUST NOT IN THE MOOD TO HAVE DEADLY PEANUTS TOSSED AT ME.

MMM... PEANUTS!
NOW I'M HUNGRY.
WHAT ON EARTH IS ZARALGAX DOING HERE ON EARTH? DIDN'T WE SEND THAT GUY BACK TO PLUTO?

I DIDN'T FLY HERE FROM THE MOON JUST TO GET POISONED BY THOSE DISGUSTING MONSTERS!

DISGUSTING MONSTERS? COME ON...
WHAT? HE CAME FROM THE MOON?

AND I ONLY GAVE YOU A RIDE BECAUSE THE BOSS SAID I TOTALLY HAD TO.

WELL, AS YOU KNOW, THE BOSS IS ALWAYS RIGHT.
SUCK-UP.

AH, THE BOSS...MY HERO! I REMEMBER WHEN HE RESCUED ME FROM THAT EXPERIMENTAL LAB TO BECOME HIS ASSISTANT...

...JUST LIKE HE RESCUED YOU BY CHANGING THE TRAJECTORY OF YOUR SHIP FROM PLUTO TO THE MOON.
?
YES, YES. I WAS THERE, REMEMBER?

HE HAD OBSERVED YOUR MISADVENTURES ON EARTH WITH THOSE TERRIBLE KIDS. HE THOUGHT YOU'D BE A GOOD ALLY TO DESTROY THAT LUNCH CLUB ONCE AND FOR ALL.
I MEAN, I TOLD HIM IT WAS A VERY TERRIBLE IDEA AND THAT YOU LOOKED LIKE A BAD GUY.
BUT HE TOLD ME THAT'S EXACTLY WHY HE WANTED YOU ON HIS TEAM. AND THAT I SHOULD KEEP MY OPINIONS TO MYSELF.
HE WASN'T WRONG!

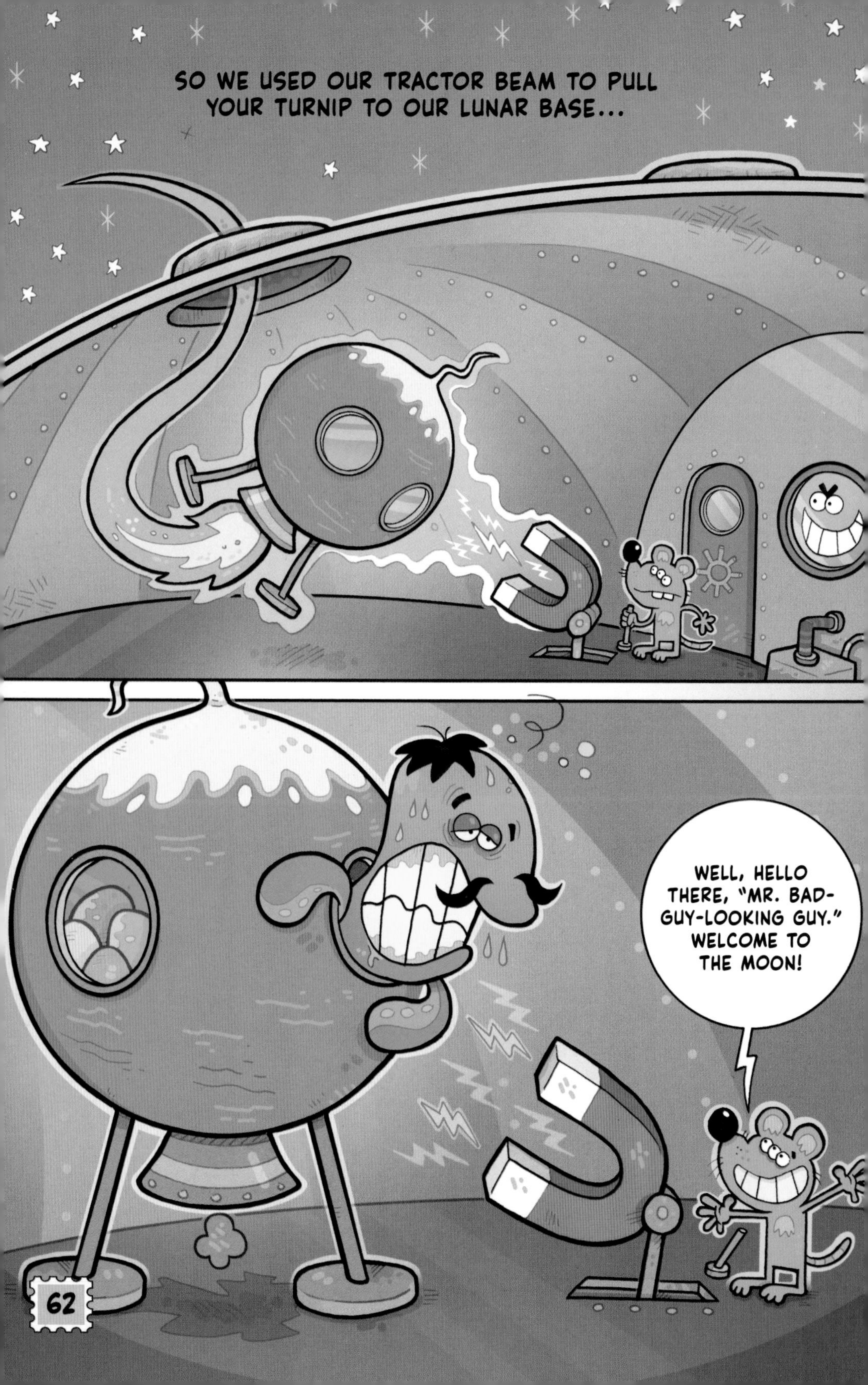
SO WE USED OUR TRACTOR BEAM TO PULL YOUR TURNIP TO OUR LUNAR BASE...
WELL, HELLO THERE, "MR. BAD-GUY-LOOKING GUY." WELCOME TO THE MOON!

YOU WERE IN PRETTY BAD SHAPE.
IS HE GONNA MAKE IT?
WITH THIS... YES!
ANTIDOTE

BUT THANKS TO OUR GENTLE CARE...
STAB!

...YOU QUICKLY BECAME YOUR OLD SELF AGAIN.
GRRR
SEE?! I TOLD YOU HE WASN'T NICE!

ZARALGAX! I WOULD AVOID EATING THAT MINUSCULE MUTANT MOUSE IF I WERE YOU.
IT'S PROBABLY TOXIC...AND ANYWAY, I HAVE SOMETHING BETTER TO OFFER YOU.
I'M A RAT!
?
WHAT WOULD YOU SAY TO GETTING SOME TASTY, TASTY VENGEANCE ON THOSE MEAN AND MONSTROUS KIDS?
HEY, I DON'T WANT TO TELL YOU WHAT TO DO, BUT THAT SEEMS LIKE A GREAT IDEA.

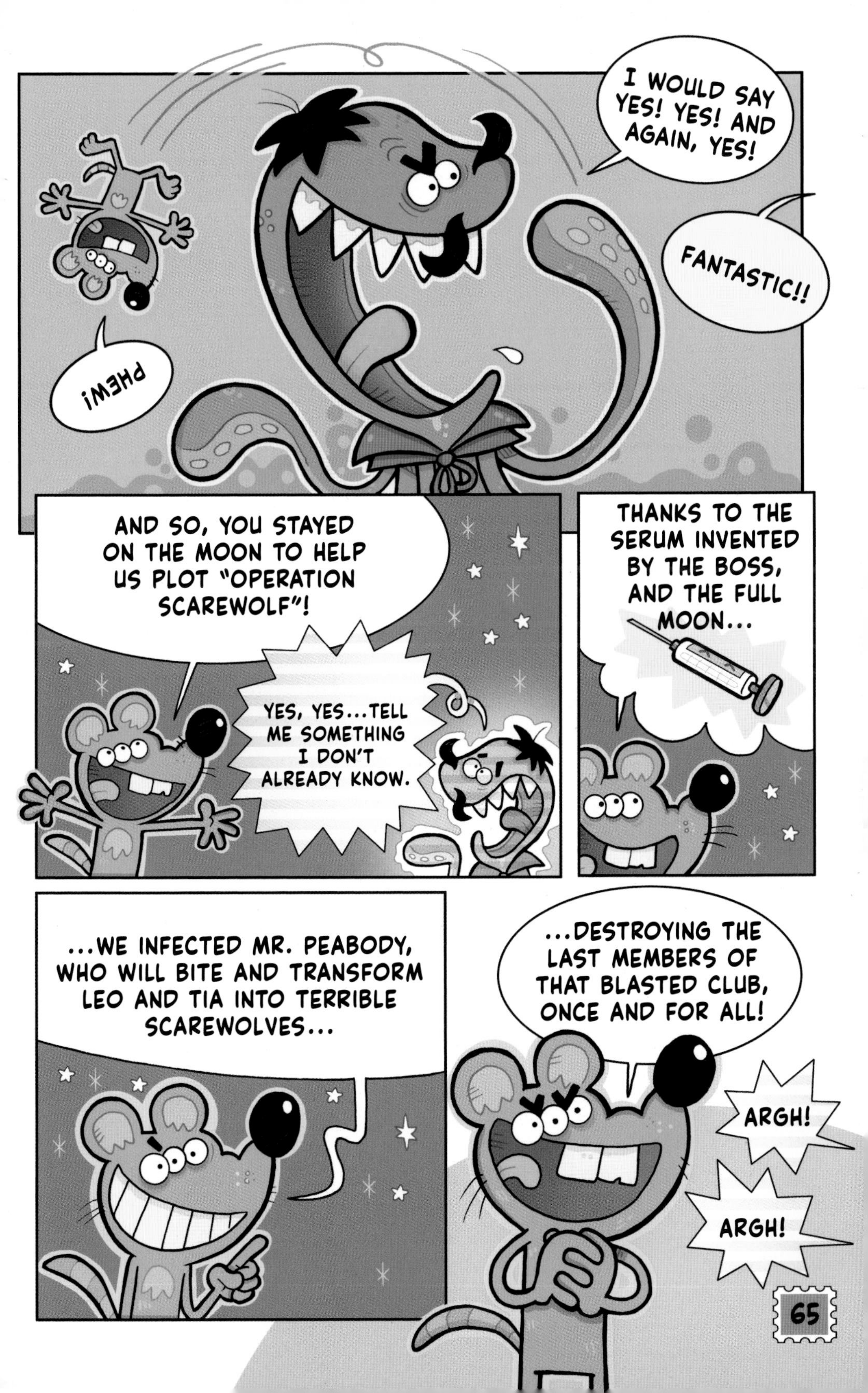
I WOULD SAY YES! YES! AND AGAIN, YES!
FANTASTIC!!
PHEW!
AND SO, YOU STAYED ON THE MOON TO HELP US PLOT "OPERATION SCAREWOLF"!
YES, YES...TELL ME SOMETHING I DON'T ALREADY KNOW.
THANKS TO THE SERUM INVENTED BY THE BOSS, AND THE FULL MOON...
...WE INFECTED MR. PEABODY, WHO WILL BITE AND TRANSFORM LEO AND TIA INTO TERRIBLE SCAREWOLVES...
...DESTROYING THE LAST MEMBERS OF THAT BLASTED CLUB, ONCE AND FOR ALL!
ARGH!
ARGH!

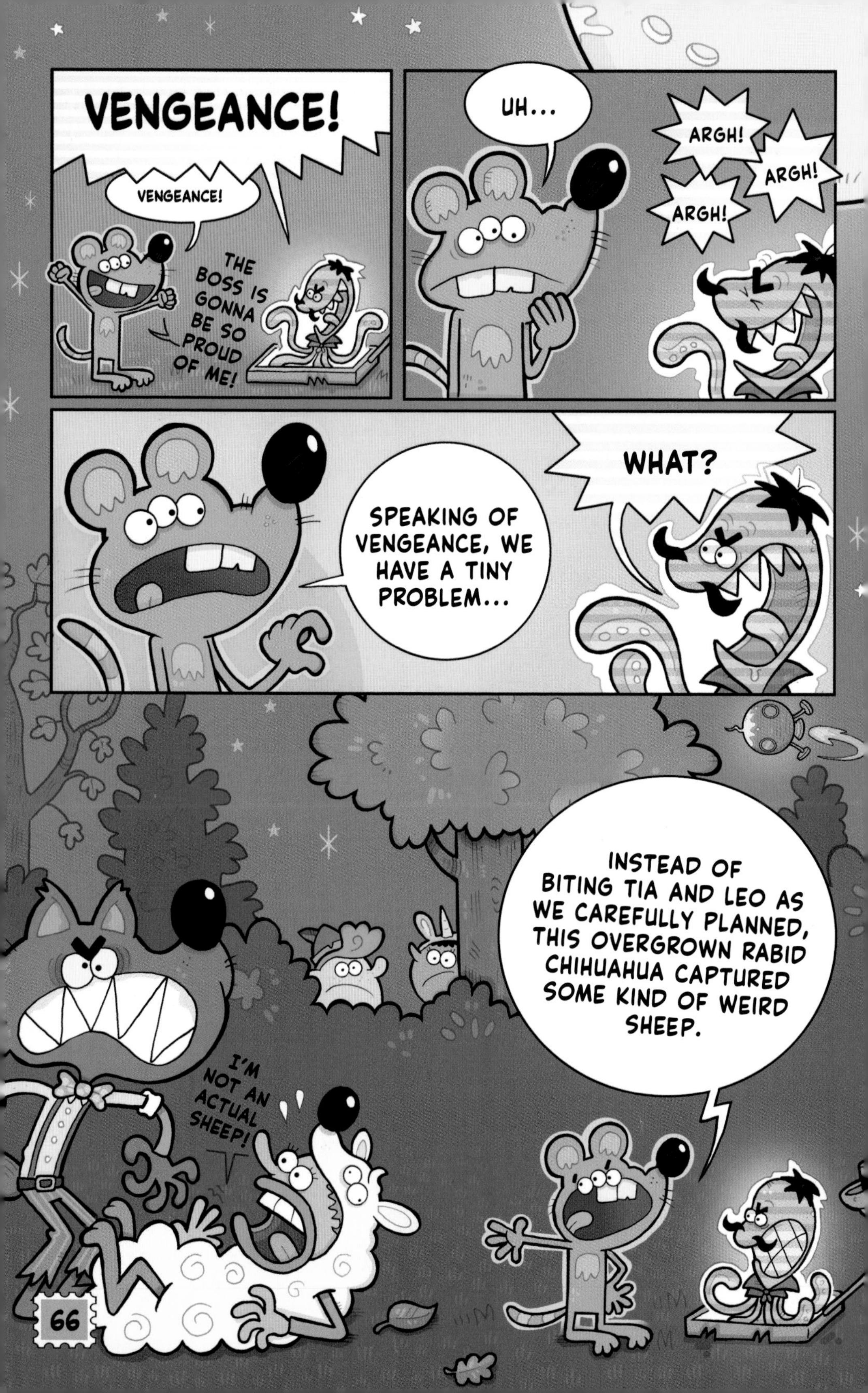
VENGEANCE!
VENGEANCE!
THE BOSS IS GONNA BE SO PROUD OF ME!
UH...
ARGH!
ARGH!
ARGH!
SPEAKING OF VENGEANCE, WE HAVE A TINY PROBLEM...
WHAT?
INSTEAD OF BITING TIA AND LEO AS WE CAREFULLY PLANNED, THIS OVERGROWN RABID CHIHUAHUA CAPTURED SOME KIND OF WEIRD SHEEP.
I'M NOT AN ACTUAL SHEEP!

HEY, SCAREWOLF! WHAT ARE YOU WAITING FOR?
STOP, OR I'LL GIVE YOU DETENTION!
GRRRRRRRR
I'LL MAKE YOU WRITE "I SHALL NOT DEVOUR THE PRINCIPAL" 100 TIMES. NEATLY!

CHOMP!
FINALLY! MORE ACTION, LESS BLABBERING!
LIKE, WHAT TOOK SO LONG?
SCENE SO HORRIFIC THAT THE AUTHOR REFUSED TO DRAW IT!
AWOOOOOO!

QUICK! THERE'S NO TIME TO MAKE A PLAN...
WE ATTACK!
AYAAAAAAA!

YAAAAAAH!

HEY! THREE-EYED MOUSE THING!
WEIRD.
I KNOW, RIGHT?
RAT!

EASY THERE, MR. PEABODY. GOOD BOY! WHAT'S UP WITH YOU? COME WITH US, FURRY BUDDY. WE'LL FIGURE OUT A WAY TO...
GRRRRR
GROOAR!

HEY, YOU...MOUSE!
I'M A RAT
A LAB RAT, FOR YOUR INFORMATION.

ARGH!
ARGH!
ARGH!

POKE
PTOING!

AAAAAAAARGH!
SORRY!

PING!

CRUNCH
BANG
BIZZZ
CRACK

PONG!

HEY, MUTANT MOUSE! HOW DO WE TURN MR. PEABODY BACK INTO A REGULAR OLD GUY?
HELP!

SONK!

BUH-BYE, SUCKERS! HEH HEH HEH.

MISSION MOSTLY ACCOMPLISHED. LET'S GET OUT OF HERE.
SEE YA, NERDS! SMELL YA LATER!
I HATE MUTANT MICE. AND TURNIPS.
AT LEAST THEY'RE GONE?

OH. WE FORGOT THE PRINCIPAL!
ARGHLB!

A LITTLE HELP HERE?

GNNNN
GNNN
A WOLF IN SHEEP'S CLOTHING. LITERALLY.

GROOOOAR

GRRR
SCREECH

THE HALLOWEEN PARTY!
I TOTALLY FORGOT!
HAL

SO...DO WE TELL THEM THAT THERE ARE WEREWOLVES IN THE WOODS?
NOPE. EVERYONE WILL PANIC.

SO...PRETEND LIKE EVERYTHING IS NORMAL?
YUP. AND SNEAK BACK TO THE CLUB.

PRETENDING LIKE EVERYTHING IS FINE...PRETENDING LIKE EVERYTHING IS FINE...PRETENDING LIKE EVERYTHING IS FINE...
IS EVERYTHING FINE, TIA?
SURE IS!

SCORE! FREE CANDY!

CANDY!

HEY, GUS!
YOU WANT CANDY?

I GOTTA GO, BUT YOU NEED TO STAY HERE WITH MOM AND DAD.
YOU'LL GET MORE CANDY WHEN I COME BACK.
CANDY!

YOU'RE EATING? NOW? SERIOUSLY!
CRUNCH! CHOMP! NOM!
WELL, OF COURSE! I FOUND CANDY.

WHAT?! THIS IS NOT THE TIME TO BE STUFFING YOUR FACE WITH CANDY!
WANT SOME?

NO! I DON'T WANT CANDY, I WANT TO DEAL WITH THE WEREWOLVES THAT ARE CURRENTLY IN THE WOODS!
RIGHT, RIGHT.
IF ONLY MR. PEABODY COULD HELP US...

IF ONLY WE KNEW MORE ABOUT WEREWOLVES.
POOR MR. PEABODY...I'VE ALMOST LOST MY APPETITE. ALMOST.

THAT'S IT!
MY LOLLIPOP?

THE BOOK!
OF COURSE!
THE JOY OF STAMPS

MR. PEABODY TOLD US THE FIRST PART IS A PRACTICAL GUIDE...

...WITH PRETTY PICTURES.
Philately

THE SUBJECTS ARE IN ALPHABETICAL ORDER. TURN TO "W."
LET'S SEE. WERERABBITS, WERESLUGS...OH, HEY! WEREUNICORNS. TIA, YOU'D BE INTO THOSE. AH, HERE WE GO. WEREWOLVES.

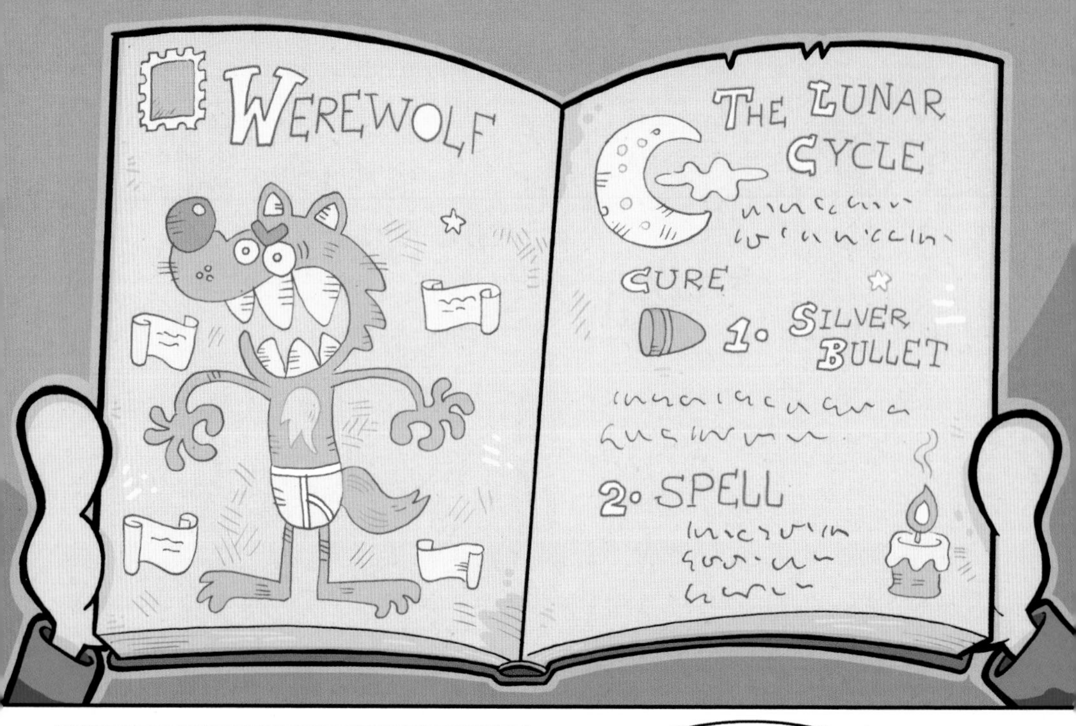
WEREWOLF
THE LUNAR CYCLE
CURE
1. SILVER BULLET
2. SPELL

ACCORDING TO THE BOOK, THERE ARE THREE WAYS TO GET RID OF A WEREWOLF.

THE FIRST IS A SILVER BULLET...
WE DON'T HAVE A GUN...

BUT I HAVE A BOW!
TA-DA!

BUT WE DON'T HAVE ANY SILVER!
I HAVE A SILVER QUARTER.

LET'S MOVE ON. THE NEXT SUGGESTION IS TO DO A PROTECTION SPELL. EASY-PEASY.

WE DRAW A CIRCLE, STAND IN IT, AND SAY THE SPELL FIVE TIMES.
LOOK, WE EVEN HAVE CHALK RIGHT HERE!

BUT WE'RE NOT TRYING TO PROTECT OURSELVES! WE WANT TO SAVE THE PRINCIPAL, THE PEOPLE AT THE PARTY AND MR. PEABODY!
RIGHT. SHOULD I DRAW A CIRCLE ON YOUR FOREHEAD JUST IN CASE?
OR A MOUSTACHE

THE THIRD CURE IS MOON DUST.
THAT'S NOT ANY BETTER.

HOW ARE WE GOING TO GET TO THE MOON?
IF THE SPACE TURNIP WAS STILL HERE, WE COULD STEAL IT.

IS NASA GOING THERE ANY TIME SOON?
NOPE...
...AND WE NEED TO ACT NOW!

UH...CAN WE MAKE MOON DUST?

MAYBE THERE'S SOME RIGHT HERE IN OUR SECRET CLUB HIDEOUT?
GOOD IDEA. THERE'S SO MUCH TOTALLY COOL STUFF HERE.

THAT'S WHAT I WAS SAYING THIS MORNING. WE COULD HAVE SHOWN SO MANY THINGS AT...

...THE SCIENCE FAIR...
CLINK

TIA! THIS MORNING AT THE SCIENCE FAIR, THERE WAS A BOOTH THAT HAD...

FIFTEEN SECONDS LATER...
MOON ROCKS
THERE ARE LOTS!
YAY!

AND THEY LOOK VERY DUSTY. HEY, WHERE DID ALL THAT CANDY GO?
OOPS. I MEANT TO SAVE SOME FOR GUS. BUT WE CAN USE THIS TO CARRY THE ROCKS.

WHAT ARE WE SUPPOSED TO DO WITH THESE?
OH, WE'LL CHUCK THEM! I BROUGHT MY SLINGSHOT.
CHUCK THEM?
MAKE A TEA?
MASH THEM AND SPRINKLE?
YOU'RE SO PREPARED.
THE PLAN IS SIMPLE: WE GO BACK TO THE WOODS AND WHEN THE WEREWOLVES OPEN THEIR JAWS, WE'LL POP A MOON ROCK RIGHT IN THERE.

GREAT! WE'LL USE THE SLINGSHOT FOR THE BIGGER ROCKS...
...AND A STRAW FOR THE SMALLER ONES!

SO, HOW DO WE GET THEM TO OPEN THEIR JAWS?
DON'T WORRY, THEY'LL OPEN THEIR MOUTHS PRETTY WIDE WHEN THEY TRY TO BITE US.
UH...OKAY. GREAT.

WE'LL SNEAK OUT THIS WAY SO NO ONE SPOTS US.

SEE ANYONE?

NOPE. IT LOOKS GOOD. THE COAST IS ALL CLEAR...

CANDY!

GUS!
WHERE DID YOU
COME FROM?
HEY,
GUS!
CANDY!

SORRY, THERE
ISN'T ANY LEFT.
SOMEBODY ATE
IT ALL...
CANDY
BYE-BYE?

IT'S ONLY
ROCKS...
...AND
YOU CAN'T
EAT ONE OF
THOSE.

GO FIND MOM
AND DAD BEFORE
THEY START
TO WORRY.

CANDY!
WE'LL
BE BACK
SOON!
QUICK!
BEFORE
IT'S TOO
LATE!

PASS ME A ROCK...

I SHOULD'VE BROUGHT SOMETHING OTHER THAN A STRAW.

WHERE ARE THEY?
MAYBE I SHOULD HAVE DRESSED UP AS LITTLE RED RIDING HOOD.
GOOD EVENING, WEREWOLVES!
WOULD YOU CARE TO COME EAT US?

AAAAOOOOOO!

GROOAR!

COME ON,
LITTLE PEBBLE,
GET IN THERE!

OH NO...
WHERE'S THE
PRINCIPAL?

GRRR

GROAR
PTING!
COME ON, LEO!
HA HA!

?
AHHHHHH!
QUICK, SHOOT!
PTOUP!
?

ARGH! IT'S NOT WORKING!
MOVE OVER, LET ME TRY!
?
CRACK!
NO!

ROOAAR

CHOMP!
LEO!

OH NO! THE MOON ROCKS!

GRRRR
GRRRR

AAAOOOOOO!
OH NO--LEO! MR. PEABODY! STOP THAT, BOTH OF YOU! IT'S ME, TIA!

GRRRR
AHHHH!
CHOMP!

GRR

AWOOOOOOO!
?
GRRR
GRRR
MMMM

GRRRRRR
ARE OUR HEROES DOOMED? WILL THIS BE THE WORST PLEASANT VALLEY HALLOWEEN BASH IN HISTORY? I GUESS YOU'LL HAVE TO WAIT UNTIL BOOK 3 TO FIND OUT...
THE END
AUTHOR

THIS ADVENTURE WAS BROUGHT TO YOU BY:
DUSTY OLD MOON ROCKS
PERFECT IN HERBAL TEAS!
DAZZLINGLY SUBTLE AND ELEGANT AS JEWELLERY!
BLING BLING
FABULOUS AS HOME DECOR!
HUNDREDS OF USES!
DUSTY OLD MOON ROCKS, ALWAYS FRESH AND SAFE.*
*NOT RECOMMENDED FOR CHILDREN UNDER THREE OR WEREWOLVES.

JUST KIDDING...IT'S NOT THE END. YET.
THERE'S STILL HOPE!
GRRRR

CANDY?

NO CANDY?

WAAH!
?

GRRRR

?

BAD DOG!
SIT!

GULP!

POOF!

LEO!
NO CANDY!

GROOOAR

GRRRR

GULP
GULP
GULP
GULP
GULP

POOF!
POOF!
POOF!

TIA!
UH...
YEAH!
AHHH!

ARE YOU ALL RIGHT, MADAM PRINCIPAL?

OH MY. WHAT JUST HAPPENED?
IT IS AT ONCE VERY SIMPLE...

...AND INCREDIBLY COMPLICATED.
MAY I ACCOMPANY MADAM BACK TO THE PARTY?
OF COURSE, KIND SIR.

MR. PEABODY? THE PRINCIPAL? EWW.

YOU THINK HE'LL TELL HER ABOUT THE CLUB?
I HOPE SO. THAT WOULD MAKE THINGS EASIER. FEWER DETENTIONS, MAYBE?

WELL, THAT WAS KIND OF FUN!
FUN? MORE LIKE A BRUSH WITH DISASTER.
LATER, GATORS!
CANDY!

WHAT NOW?
BACK TO THE PARTY!
NO, I MEAN ABOUT THE SUPERVILLAINS ON THE MOON.
WHAT WE ALWAYS DO: IMPROVISE...
...AND BE SUPER COOL!
I WONDER WHO THE "BOSS" THEY WERE TALKING ABOUT IS.
YEAH. HE'S PROBABLY NOT THE WORLD'S MOST NICEST PERSON.
AND HE OWES ME A PAIR OF SNEAKERS.

BIG HALLOWEEN
CANDY!

I'VE EXPLAINED EVERYTHING TO OUR CHARMING PRINCIPAL...
AND DON'T WORRY, YOUR SECRET CLUB WILL REMAIN... A SECRET.
THIS IS ALL SO EXCITING!
SHALL WE DANCE?
I WAS ABOUT TO ASK YOU THE SAME THING!

HUH.
LOOK AT THAT.
WHO KNEW?

GRRRRR!
?
?
?

AHHHH!
EEEEK!

WOW! I KNEW MY COSTUME WAS GOOD, BUT NOT THAT GOOD! STAY COOL, KIDS!
HA! HA! HA! HA! HA! HA! HA! HA!
YAAA!

A

BIG HALLOWEEN BASH
THE END

I'M SURE THE BOSS WILL BE HAPPY!
ARGH!
I HAVE FINALLY EXACTED MY REVENGE ON THAT RIDICULOUS CLUB!
ARGH!

I HOPE WE GET A PARTY. WE DESERVE A PARTY!
WITH CHEESE PUFFS...
...AND THOSE LITTLE SANDWICHES WITH THE CRUSTS CUT OFF!

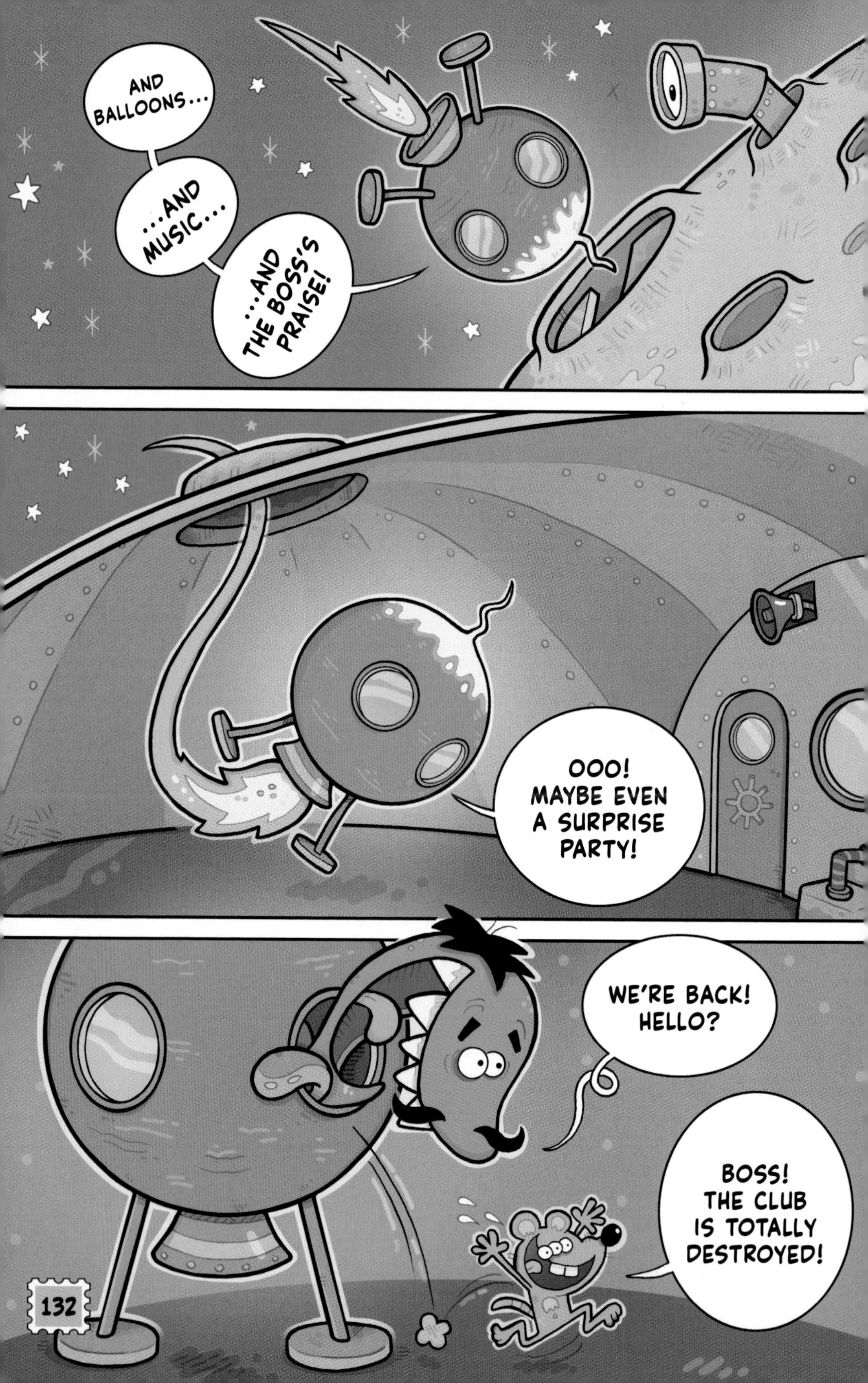
AND BALLOONS...
...AND MUSIC...
...AND THE BOSS'S PRAISE!
OOO! MAYBE EVEN A SURPRISE PARTY!
WE'RE BACK! HELLO?
BOSS! THE CLUB IS TOTALLY DESTROYED!

WHAT DO YOU MEAN "DESTROYED"? THE CLUB IS STILL THERE. ITS MEMBERS ARE HAVING FUN AND DANCING! YOUR MISSION WAS A COMPLETE AND UTTER FAILURE! WE HAVE TO START OVER!
NO PARTY?
?
TIME TO MOVE ON TO SERIOUS BUSINESS...

PLAN B!
HA! HA! HA! HA! HA! HA! HA! HA!

FIND OUT WHAT HAPPENS NEXT IN BOOK 3!
EVEN SCARIER THREATS!
SUSPENSE!

ACTION!
SNOW!
REVELATIONS!
EWW!
MAGIC!
HAVE YOU READ BOOK 1?
IT CAME FROM THE BASEMENT
SCHOLASTIC
EXCELLENT WITH SPACE KETCHUP!

DOM PELLETIER

DOMINIQUE PELLETIER LIVES IN THE QUEBEC COUNTRYSIDE WITH HIS FAMILY. THEY HAVE THREE CHICKENS, TWO PONIES, A CAT AND A LAZY DOG. AND SOMETIMES MICE BECAUSE THE CAT IS ALSO LAZY.

GROWING UP, DOMINIQUE WANTED TO BE EITHER A BASEBALL PLAYER OR A COMIC BOOK ARTIST, BUT SINCE HE DIDN'T UNDERSTAND THE RULES OF BASEBALL (AND STILL DOESN'T), HE DECIDED TO GO WITH DRAWING. DOMINIQUE HAS ILLUSTRATED MORE THAN ONE HUNDRED BOOKS. THE LUNCH CLUB SERIES IS THE FIRST THAT HE HAS ALSO WRITTEN.